CW00516224

# Contents

# Walking the Long Road Home

## Intro

Hi boys and girls, Okay
I'm going to give you a
new intro... Let's see how
this goes

« Get out of my head !
You're not real !

Demons, shadows, voices of
the night ! Go away !

Sorry sorry, I didn't mean
that. Look let's start
again...

« You said i was tired.

You said i'm no longer the
man I once was ? »
« Yes I get that. I guess
that must be true. I'm
older. I've matured. Like
fine cheese I've added
flavour, strength and
character. And like wine
i've turned, a bit sour. A
bit sharp, difficult to
swallow. And leaves you
feeling a little bit
funny, after you've dealt
with me.

So do i regret her ? Do I
regret them> ? Do i
regret, throwing my life
away.

Damn they say break a man,
and he will never be the
same/

I've been broken so many
times, I am kind of
BROKEN.

But you know, i do have
commitments. My pledge to
the truth is accurate, as
it is deep AND sincere.
But likewise, the pen of
the editor, has to
hesitate, if not, say slow
down, and double take,
some of my more
inappropriate outbursts.
Specifically I can't say
stuff that will get me a
divorce. Or look bad on my
kid. That's about it.

Oh yes, and I'm going to
let rip now... (good luck)

# Chapter One

You are what you want.
{ed. and by that I mean ; you *can* be}
You are who you want to be. The
books you ceruse, the television
series you watch

The people you meet. The music you
listen to. The lovers you leave
behind. Those you kissed. And those
you didn't.

It's all there. You are who were were
meant to be.
You were born to have a place in this
world.

Your tears water the flowers of the
future/ And they were borrowed
from them. And they were gifted to
you, from the seas of our elders/

The world is ten thousand years old. Maybe it is ten million ? I've got no idea. Okay maybe i should believe what i am told. That the scientific community has a consensus, which finds congruence in it's accuracy. Yeah maybe. I mean I learnt how to stand on my own two feet, to make my own friends.

I learnt that myself. No-body taught me that. Same as I learnt how to play the guitar. How to tune my guitars. How to master Xbox games (from final fantasy 7,9, elder scrolls 5 skyrim, fallout 4, grand theft auto online, and now call of duty black ops Cold War). They say don't look back. But it's fun to walk two steps forward, and one back. That's how you dance right ? Well do the cha-cha at least ! Hehe.

Plus it helps to look out for enemies on the street. Specifically bad guys trying to sucker punch you.

I mean if you don't have any enemies, then no one, will try to do this to you. Doesn't matter.

So what do you do ? Annihilate them ? Er no. Sorry this life isn't a game. You have to play by the rules.

If you've never been in trouble with the law, you've got a chance. A chance to mess-up. Just don't push it too far. But I'm digressing.
.....

Don't let the devil control your destiny.

Wrest power of that beast. Win back the day.

Don't believe the liars.

They have another agenda. They will
steal your money, your goodwill,
your spirit. One day we will die.
Even those of us who live for a
century (100 years), will one day
return to our maker.

And when we do, we will stand on
those pearly steps, and forced to
account for all of our thefts. All of
our lies, our indescretions, our
mistakes.

Will he let us through ? Have your
actions provided a blessing or a
tragedy. Have you saved more souls
then you have damned ?

Or is your footprint a communist's
dream. Full of self empowerment,
but bereft of truth, of sympathy, of
truth.

None of us have seen the lord. Even those who claim to have died, haven't/ Because once you step though those pearly gates, there is no going back.

We need to be accountable for. To face up to our deamons. To retrieve what treasures we can, and also to share.

This life wasn't the only one. We steal a minute of our time of Earth, from our forefathers, and mothers, and the children yet to come. One day they will all end.

One day, if hope is to be believed, mankind will find a way to make inters galaxial star travel a reality. I know it seems a long way off now, but much as the microchip would have seemed an imposibilty to us, a hundred years ago. So too who knows what the future will hold for us.

Star ship travel, yes i believe we *may* be able to crack that one.
If we can find out how to enter time warps, maybe using the power of black holes, time travel/relativity, er the micro scope of the atom and intergenerational quatum excellence, the scope of the internet, the strength of harmony music and rythm, and the strength of the perfect chess game. The perfect victory. The excellence of a kiss, of a child, of making one, and holding it in.

So what now ? Where do we go from here ? Are our times limited to a single sigh. A fight, a fall, a mistake. A penny a pound.

Writing is my destiny. You do realise that right ? This is my mark on the world. My statement to my children, and excellence in its' purist form.

I would like to spend a little time discussing games for a minute, but before we go there, let's just look again at what is possible ? I mean I think star ship travel may become possible in the future. And the atom, still holds a great range of quantum potential. But time travel ? I somehow have great doubts and reservations, that this can ever be fully realised. That's not to say that progress, can't be made here ? Just the limits of reality, for example the fact that, by it's very definition, time can not go backwards, remains something of a firewall, unmovable barrier i'm afraid.

Einstein taught us some great ideas
with his Theories of Relativity,
including $E=Mc^2$, and special
relativity, including that the speed of
light is the fastest speed possible.
Even though I know a faster one,
which is what *IS*, which is the realm
of God, and not man.

But Man was made in god's image.
And so too was woman. Who was
taken from one of man's ribs/. And
do I believe that ? Let us not
question faith any more. We need to
trust, and put our petty disbelief
aside for a minute.

So with creation, all is possible. With
time, and attention, we can
overcome our struggles, and move
forwards. One day we will all die.
Even those of us who are destined
for the stars, must first walk on the
earth. Swim with the fishes, sway

with the trees, and sleep with the sloths. It was all there for us. She gave her all. And we took it, time and time again. We took it so many times, that there was nothing left to give. She was left unable to walk. Unable to sleep. In a wheel chair ? And we gave her ? Nine months in the womb, and a life time of hope. A new life. A baby.

Did the contact remain ? How many children did you have Boris ? John ? Barry ? How many were you able to support, and how many did you leave to fend for themselves. Growing up life without a father. Were you forgiven, for giving the mother a precious gift, and then hiding away, like the coward they always said you were ?

I don't know. I mean I think man and women to go together nicely, even if only for a short period of time.

This time I want to keep the narrative special. Not to share it with anyone, until the script is complete. And then release it under my own brand, as I did my first five books.

We are making progress. And that's one of the beauties of fiction, right ? You are able to capture a moment of crystal beauty, forever, in that moment he was made. The moment, she was made ? The power of Allah/Jehovah, of Jesus. Of Sophia the goddess of wisdom, of Mother Nature, who gives our plants sometime to drink, and a home to stay at.

Games are fun, zombies are good, good to shoot, preferably in the face, or strenum (centre chest). I'm a great believer that we need to work hard, to follow our aptitudes as they are presented us. To do what we can, with what we are given. If you can work, and earn a living, go for it. I have struggled to hold down work. Even with these voluntary roles, they remain elusive, for the few months or so. But we keep on trying. The royal we. The Queen and I. I actually wrote her Majesty a Christmas card last Christmas. I just thought she might need cheering up. With the loss of her life partner, Prince Philip for example ? And did she get it ? I don't know. But I tell you what, I have seen a picture of her smiling recently, which was good to see. Because she did look a bit sat prior to that, as I'm sure you can understand.

I would like to finish today's tale with a mention of the games I have recently played. Well games I have beastcd, and completed, include Grand Theft Auto V (five), The Elder Scrolls 4 Skyrin, and Fallout 4, all on the Xbox, all with over a thousand in game play hours. I am now playing mainly between GTA online, and Call of Duty //Black Ops 3, the first of which is a RPG/ first person open world game, the second being a high tech shooter. Actually something I have been working on recently for call of duty blops 3 is a transcript of the hidden campaign mission hidden prologues, which can be revealed with some time, dedication, and a high powered android/smart phone. Any way today I finished recording the fourth hidden text, from this game, which, although still quite jumbled and confusing, does nevertheless give some back story, and colour to the main campaign missions on this game. See links below for the meat to this endeavour, so far at least...

cheers !

## The Happy Princess 2

«Today » The Happy Princess declared,
« Today is My day ! »
« It is the day for all of the mothers',
all of the daughter's, all of the friends, and all of the lovers.
« No longer do you have to go to bed lonely, thinking of what might have been.
« How differently your life might have turned out if you had kissed a *different* partner, fallen in love with

someone else, or studied a different degree.

« Count your blessings. I am here for you. All of you.

Do you remember when i wrestled that tiger, bested that daemon, defeated that ogre ?
Yes I did it for me, for my mum, for my step dad. It was a personal struggle, which made me suffer at the time. And yes i did suffer in silence. Much as our cat, Daisy, also suffered. And one day paid the ultimate price

But unlike Daisy, I survivied We survived. My bloody nation survived. Yes and guess what we're still surviving. My God is surviving. And people and living, we're living good. We've got books. We've got music. We've got everything.

But if I EVER hear you say you are going to take this away from me again, If i ever see you have been creeping, without my bloody agreement, I will bloody do my bloody nut.

I have taken this rubbish from you and this bloody country to too bloody long. It needs to stop, and it Needs to stop NOW ! Okay> Got that ?

Sorry.


## The Happy Princess Reboot

The next day Mich had made up her mind. She had had enough. She was fed up of all the back biters, liars, and criminals in the United

Kingdom. She was going home (back to Africa).

So she brought her and her little sister, and mother a ticket, then a short four hour plane ride later, and they were home !

HELLO AFRICA ! They shouted, as they got off the plane. And people smiled and laughed at her, when they saw her. She had made it ? Gone from the mother land, to the emerald isles, and returned home in one piece.

And she loved it. Her aim ? To reunite the two homelands, that of her mother, and her father ? And could she do it ? As a Princess, it was her regal right to do so ! Hell, her duty you might say ?

Bring together the children of the world, all of the lost, and sad. Bring

them together, as one. One family,
under one sun.

And boy what a sun ?! It was too hot
for her. She tried to avoid spending
long times under him, so as to avoid
getting burned. Under him the sun i
mean, Excuse my french. Personally
I don't like using sun lotion,
although I realise many people do
disagree with me on that one.


And in Kenya, Michelle, saw all of
her old friends, Micky and Ricky,
Teacher Anne's twin sons, both of
whom had grown into fighting
young men now, with the heat.

Daisy the old Kikuyu Kenyan
Warrioress, who still put the rubbish
bins out, in the hospital she lived,
and worked at (without pay),
Chiromo Lane.

And Michael and Dr Njenga, both medical doctor's from that same chinic.

Then after a couple of weeks abroad, she decided that it was time to come home. She did love seeing the Kenyans, and it was refreshing eating a sugar and chemical free diet, which is in fact pretty much the opposite of the UK diet, which you only fully appreciate, once you have tried it.

But she didn't like the unequality of the sexes over there. For example how some men, still think that they are better than the women, even though it was the women who have to hand wash the clothes ? This is still backwards, she thought ?

And so did she prefer Kenya of Britain ?

Hold on I will ask her...

She says « Kenya, because it's warm, and people are nice »

God bless.

## Games and Spies

Next I want to share some insights in to the games, I've played and loved over the years.

I actually completed Final Fantasy 7, 9 and X-2 on the playstation, which was something. In order to get on with that game, I found I had to enter a trance when playing it. And that was the way I was able to master the hundreds of hours of dedication, needed to tackle it.

I actually started gaming on the PC before the consoles really took off. Completing a couple of tours of duty campaigns on the story mode, at different difficulty levels. I found the challenge of shooting down Tie fighters, well the first is the hardest. Once you get the knack of it, it gets a lot eaiser, and fun. I even took out some Imperial Star Destroyers, although I don't think I was ever able to take down the Death Star/

But when the Xbox 360, and later Xbox One came out, well by that time I left the PC and Playstation gaming, and haven't really looked back.

So more recent games i have throughly rinsed and completed include THe Elder Scrolls 5 Skyrim, Grand Theft Auto 5, and Fallout 4. Who could ever forget the classic line of, « Boss, there's another settlement needs our help », from Fallout 4, or « I used to be an explorer like you, til i took an arrow to the knee ! » from Skyrim, hehe. Happy times.

So bringing us right up to the preset, the two games i seem to be engaging with most at present, are GTA 5/Online, and also Call of Duty Black Ops 3, mainly Zombies mode. Actually Call of Duty Black Ops 1 had a fascinating Easter Egg, at the beginning of the game, which started with the moment of a special forces man screaming, prior to/as he was, being torgtured.

Well with the correct wrigggling of the control pad sticks, and mashing of the buttons, and it was actually possible to take control of this hero, and break free from your bonds. Then after this, if you walked around to the back of the setup, you could actually sit down and log in to an old DOS based computer terminal. Which was linked in to some mainframe. And from there you could read the emails, and view the pictures/here the sound bytes of a number of secret service agents, ranging from Mason, the main protagonist in the game, right the way through to the president. And these character's also had encoded numbers linked to their accounts, which if you hacked the code, revealed secret messages/

Plus where was actually another mainframe server or two, it was possible to hack in to. And i managed to crack these, although I seem to remember they eluded less information than the first one, actually server three i wasn't able to get anything out of at all. But it was all good fun. And It's also good sharing our findings with the internet.

So fast forward to today, and playing Black Ops 3, also has a Safehouse\ with a terminal, and a secret. But this time, I found the secret is not from the terminal, altough granted there is some juicy stuff in there, I found the proper meat on this piece of fruit, to be taken from the campaign missions.

I am about half way through the main story missions. Which so far seem to be a somewhat confused secret services, intelligence and soldier based brief, ranging from Eygpt to the Far and Middle East. I'm loving playing it though. And have even completed the first mission, on realistic, which is uber hard, because two shots and you're dead.

Anyway, just before the commencement off these missions, and for a few seconds, very quickly a few pages of text scroll of the screen. I was intially unable to make any sense of this. But now I have brought a powerful phone, and I am actually able to record this text, with my video camera, then play it back, frame by frame, and record the text, more or less. I say more or less, because it is still quite tricky to do. And i still struggled with some of this detail. Especially with the fourth mission, so far. But the meat it shows, are mission records, after mission reports, and facts. Ranging from the attribution of blame, to certain officers, or their absolvement of this, and the name of four target individuals, who equally have the blame of murders, and the betrayal of top secret classified information, laid at their feet.

I know this is only a game, but it is so well done, from the person to person gun fighting, the open map camping and target acquisition placements, of the different maps and their terrain (personally I loved the market place cubby holes and circular layout of the Tokyo/China map, and not to forget the Zombie mode. Hell My wife even says that Look like a zombie, which is funny, even if I may bare some resemblance to one. Hehe.

Oh dead. On that note I'm going to sign off. Oh yes, and finally a quick hint, in case any of you ever do come across the undead in a call of duty game, quickly shoot it in the head, or face preferably ! Echo out.

# Childhood

Okay, let's go back. Forget when my parent's first met. I can't remember that.

Let's go back to my earliest memory as a child. Which is being told to, and obeying, being sat in the dunce's chair in nursery school. And this happened to me on more than one occasion. Then at primary school, I had no friends' In fact I was the only white boy in class for year five. And just when i nearly made a friend at school, they moved me. Also I do remember reading a book, in a few days, maybe a week. The Twits by Roald Dahl, certainly a classic, by any means. Even though my teacher didn't believe me, and got me to read it again, and again.

I mean this obsession with reading, didn't really hit me again, until my year 11 Gsces. I'd basically flunked the mocks, and got me like straight Ds, apart from Maths and Science, which I got Bs for. But at that time, a Mrs P, a very kind and listening teacher, gave me a book to read, on GCSE exam technique, so then, with that under my belt, I was able to focus, and fully concentrate on revising for my exams. Which I did with a vengeance. Actually If anything I revised too much. But because I had very few, next to no friends, to hand out with, I didn't mind this geeky profile. I hoped it would never end.

The i got run over, and it very nearly did.

Fast forward twenty five years, and I've not finished university, done two tours of hospital regime change duty, and now been in my own flat for four years. Okay my wife and daughter no longet life with me, but they still visit, so it's not all bad.

I think I may have told you before but I have really recently been getting in to my games, once again. Call of Duty black ops 3, and Grand theft auto five. Both which have lucid and lush graphics, which makes playing them a dream. And my conquests' today ? Well on GTA online, I managed to rob two crates from a cargo depot near my nightclub, which isn't bad seeing as there were like another three or four guys trying to do the same. I got out with two, so yep that wasn't bad. And for COD ? I recorded, and then transcribed another script from the campaign mode, this one finishing with a personal comment from John Taylor (I think). And American

Special Force's commando. This was the sixth one I've done. Actually I've really enjoyed working with this material. And I'm somethings struggling to make sense of it. Expecially when there are words, or even whole sentences corrupted. But I'm getting better at recording with my phone, so I am doing a better job with these transcripts. I'm not going to copy the whole text, for reason's of plaigerism, but just the final sentences :

Hendrick 's being an officer in the game, and the LNO being Rachel Kane. But suffice to say that he Doesn't have romantic feelings for her. He just wanted to clear that up.

So yes that about wraps up my work for today. I hope you have enjoyed the journey with me so far, and hopefully if you stick with me as we progress. you can share my thoughts, emotions and experiences, with me in this way. So thanks !

## JoJo the Killer

« Hi young man » the black uniformed man, began.
« What is your' name ? »
« JoJo »
« And what do you do for a living ? »
« I kill people »
« Whaat ? »
« Sorry i mean to say, I can people. I do have the power. I learnt it some years ago. Although i have never actually killed any-one in a fight. I normally end up worse than the perp. I'm engaging with »
« Go-on »
« Yes and I also have a killer front punch. Call it a push jab, but I can disrupt an enemies line of center,

right down to his spine, if i catch
them right »
« And did you catch them ? »
« Yes, on two occasions, the first was
when this homeless guy mugged me
on the way from the gym, and i gave
chase a brought him down, then saw
him in a wheel chair afterwards »
« And the other one ? »
« Oh it was my mate Joey, i just got a
bit carried away in a local coffee
house, and did this Guillotine on
him, and he said afterwards, it really
hurt, like i had actually dislocated
one of his spinal vertabrae, and he's
actually scared of me now. God bless
him. »
« So you've never actually killed
anyone with it »
« Or with a knife »
« Have you ever stabbed or shot
anyone ? »
« Stabbed, no, shot, yes. I shot my
dad with an air pistol (on the arm)
over twenty years ago, which was a

the final straw in him moving out
from the family home, way back
when »
« But you didn't kill him »
« No »
« So who did you kill ? »
« Well i'm not really in a position to
talk about this, but twice dropped
old people in a nursing home, one
who then later went on to fall and
die, so you could say I had a factor in
his death ? »
« And why did you do that ? »
« It wasn't purposeful, it was an
accident. I had just come out from an
all night police custody, which
meant my stamina was shot. And i
was trying to give him a shave, in a
wheelchair, but i misjudged holding
it, and lost grip, and he fell
backwards, and banged his head. So
murder, no, manslaughter, not
entirely. Cos as I also said, he did
have other falls as well. Anyway if
they lock me up because of that, they

will be taking a father away from his daughter, and a husband from his wife. I've been honest with you. I try to be honest, it is what keeps me happy and enables me to, stand in front of Michael and Gabriel, at the gates of heaven and offer them at my word. »

« Plus i asked the poor gent if he was okay after, and he said he was, not that this makes it alright. »

« Well there is that then »

« Yes ta ».

## An Honest Woman

« I met your mother over twenty years ago at college. She is a couple of years younger than me, and a stunner then. Not than she isn't now »

« Go on dad »

« Yes so we were both young and reckless. It's just one of the thing that time does to a human. Brings on memories, grey hairs and wrinkles.

Any way we were both studying for our AVCE in Health and Social Care, at Derby College, Wilmorton. Which actually happens to be where i live now ! »
« You live in a college campus ? »
« No kid, this flat i now rent, well it, this estate, was brought from the college, not long after i left. They sold the site, and knocked it down, and brought another couple of areas, some-where else »
« How do you know all of this ? »
« It is common knowledge »

« Any-way tell me more about mum, the first time you met her, what did she smell like »

« She smelt nice. She was clean. She always has been. And I remember she used a perfume some other girls, or should that be, young women, from out class used at the time. Fruity, and female smelling, if there can be such a thing »

« So did she make you a man, then ? »
« Don't be silly. That came later.

Anyway, she actually left short of finishing her first year. I remember she went back to Kenya with her aunty, and then was stranded there, as her aunt took her passport. She had no means, no passport of money, no way of getting back ! »

« So how did you make touch with her again, I mean how did you restore contact ? »
« Yes talk about walking up a mountain ! Haha. That was a

challenge. I remember getting depressed about her. Thinkining that I'd never see her again. Etc. Yada yada yada.
Any way I knew where she lived, used to live sorry, in this city. It was in the Cavendish/Littleover area. Okay, true I didn't know that area well, but we had walked back together a couple of times, to her aunty/uncles' house, so I knew enough to get back there, in one piece.

Then one day when I was feeling brave, I retraced our footsteps. I'm not sure if anyone answered the door the first time I visited. But the second time at least, her younger sister answered. And I was able to get either her mobile number or possibly her email address, and then restore contact. That was the hard part done, or so i thought.

Then a couple of times, in 2007 and 2008, I flew over, we made you, and in 2012/13 brought you girls back.

I actually had to win a big court case against the UK embassy in Kenya, Appeals hearing, with the help of a good Barrister, then we lived together in a small house in the UK, Mackworth, for a bit.

Anyway, it all became too much, from me, struggling to complete my undergraduate degree, remembering to take my medication, and not argue too much. »
« So you got your degree, you used to shout at my mum, and did you ever hit her »
« I can't remember doing then kid. »
« Please trust me on this one »
« And did anything else happen ? »
« Not that you don't already know about. Can we move on now ? »

« Fine so what next ? »
« Well I'm going to finish this book »
« It is actually going to be a best-
seller »
« Really ? »
« Hehe probably not »
« Anyway, at least it gives some
body somewhere the chance to learn
more about our story, and even
follow our footsteps, should they
want to fall in love, start a
story/narrative, or change the
world ! »
« Nice. »

# Under the Stars

Together we live our
lives. Holding on to our
loved ones. Trying to
learn from our mistakes,
build on our asset base,
and let go of our
failures.

But just as the Axis is at
the centre of wheel, a
society is only as good as
it treats its' poorest
citizens I would argue.

It is easy to bully, and
get your own way, when you
are in a position of
power.

God only knows, for all of
the years I was in the
Court of Protection,

deemed unable to manage my
own financial affairs. I
was actually homeless,
before I got my first
home. Flat even.

And then all of these
years later, I have a new
flat. And a medical
history as long as your
arm. Or as long as some
internet porn-star, haha
(inappropriate).

Anyway.

So yes there I was, bored,
and at a loss of what to
do next. I tried playing
games, but they made me
boz-eyed. I tried cooking
and eating, but my pizzas
would often come out
burnt, when I forgot to
turn the oven off, for
example.

This was many years ago
when I was still a kid.

Because what is the
definition of kid/child-
hood, and when you become
a man.

Is it when you learn to
cook, your own food. Wash
your own clothes, write a
book, author a novel,
father a kid, or lose your
virginity.

Or is it when you find
God. Give your life down
to the one who made us.
Commit your future well-
fare, to His well-fare.
Find truth in the Bible ?

Truth be told, there are
lots of Holy Books. From
the Jewish scriptures, the

Torah and the Talmud for
example, which actually
predate the evens of the
New Testament, by some
generations.

Right the way across the
spectrum to the Bhagavada
Gita, which is the Hindu
holy text. Or one of them
anyway. And actually
promoted the Indian
revolution, away from the
British. Some hundred
years earlier.

I'm not in a position to
tell you what to believe.
We all have our own life
trajectories, and
individual experiences,
which to a large extent,
determine, who *we* are.

Some of us are lucky to
fall in love. Some will

get married, many will divorce. Some will go to university, and some of those will graduate. Many will drop out prior to doing so. Be this, oft-times due to no fault of their own.

Some will have kids, others won't.

Some will enjoy television, be it films from Netflix, or tv series from Amazon Prime...

There are lots of possibilities in this life. By all means please choose to be the master of your own story. Have a dream, and stick to him, or her.

Not all of our dreams come true.

Some-times we have to let go of those we love. Some-times, possibly due to hno fault of our own, we havw to say good-bye.

Whether this is due to death, or detachment.

Makind good friends is an important skill. One that i really have become quite deft at/adapt, after all of these years I have spent locked in hospital wards.

Oh yes and I have NEVER been to jail. Don't you believe it.

I actually remember the first time I was in a

prison holding cell, and
they were looking into
moving me, so they asked
me whether I wanted to go
to a jail, or hospital. I
said « hospital » and ever
since then, that has been
my destination, on leaving
the arrest hold.

For what its worth. Which
probably isn't much.

But now I have better
access, over my money, it
just gives me freedom to
better support my loved
ones, well my wife and her
daughters at least,
without the constant worry
over money. I once had.

I'm going to wrap it up
here. Thanks for bearing
with me. I know things
haven't always been easy

for the two of us. Me the
author, inventing these
parables, and you to
silent listener, the fly
on the way.

But the fact that I do
still get down-loads and
« reads » every month. All
be it not great numbers,
but just enough to
demonstrate that there are
still people out there,
who are willing to spend
time with my
writings/literature, does
still mean a lot to me.

And when I do finally die,
be it in twenty, forty,
years, or tomorrow, I'm
hoping my books will have
made a good enough
impression at that point,
to carry my legacy
forwards, for a while yet.

That and my surviving
friends and family, and
remember the good things
about me. Which is the
most any of us can ask
for.


# A warm fuzzy feeling

But that's love right.
Your commitment to stand
by them, through thick and
thin. And then if things
fall by the way-side ?
Well you pick up the
pieces, and try again.

Rome wasn't built in a
day. And the sharpest
sword, is welded in the
hottest of fires.

Equally the strongest
relationship, is built
upon commitments, lasting
many years.

I am a hypocrit, to some
extent. In that I had her,
them, and i lost her.
But
I am still trying.

Okay, let's move things on
from here.

## Thankyou Princess

A few weeks ago I brought
myself a nice mountain
bike. It's a Trek 4900,
basically the wet-dream of
any young biking
enthusiast ! I don't even
use it for going off-road,
just riding round the

local lake/pond, close to
my house...

Okay, as I think i already
mentioned, this was the
first time I have ridden a
bike, for any significant
distance, in about twenty
years. And the first time
I ventured out, to lap the
lake ten times, I fell off
at the end. I under-
estimated the steepness of
the embankment to my
right, and ended up
throwing myself off, and
putting my arm out in the
process.

I'm pretty sure I broke
it, given the powerful
pain it gave me, keeping
me up at night for a good
two weeks after. But I
recently felt strong, and
brave enough to venture

out again. And I did ten
laps again, only this time
I didn't fall off again.
I'd say the lake, or pond
as the Canadians would
call it i am assured, is a
good 100 meters round,
probably more than that,
so ten laps is like a km,
or even a mile i would
dare say.

Actually I have had a lot
of support from the
mountain biking room on
the Reddit website, where
the majority or chatters,
were throwing praise on
me. You know this is a
really good feeling, to
get encouragement for a
new hobby, I only quite
recently started. And I
have yet to hit any
people, or ducks, thank
God.

In fact I have had to pull
a few emergency stops, two
on the first outing, and
one or two on the second.
Mainly to avoid Geese, or
there was this one family
who like just got in the
way, on my first trip out.
I was like, okay I will
slow down, and stop, to
avoid hitting you.

Which was just as well.

This whole learning to
ride a bike again, by
throwing myself in the
fire, and building up my
action, strength and
endurance, really is a
blessing. The fact is that
I know the lake well now.
Me and dad used to go
there, on a regular basis,
to feed the ducks and
geese-lings (baby geese).

Oh my god those geeselings
and baby ducks were so
cute. They used to huddle
together to conserve
warmth. Then one day they
all disappeared. I'm not
sure if some poachers, or
lake wardens decided they
needed to be culled, or if
they just grew up. I mean
I can actually see the
sense in culling them, so
as to preserve the food
left for the other birds.
But I wouldn't like to
have been the one to do
it.

It's like some years ago,
when one of my American
internet mates, Song2 I
think his name was, told
me that he was tasked with
taking out a horse. And he
had to do this with a
hammer. Poor horse. And

poor guy. This must have been horrific.

That was from a MMA website I have long since been evicted from. Adding another site to the list. I have now been banned from a couple of pubs, over ten websites. A quite a few martial arts clubs as well. What is it they say ? Word spreads fast. Damn . I'm just trying now to stay on the right side of the Law (police), and Mental Health Act (hospitals).

Actually I have a meeting coming up in under a couple of weeks, where I am hoping to ask for another reduction of my meds, so I'm hoping she will agree to this.

Evidence to the fore ;
I have been reasonably
well for the last year,
since my last meds were
reduced. And definitely
feel a lot better, now I
have switched from the
injections (depots) to the
tablets, which I self
medicate.

Ok there is the problem of
adherance, because I do
sometimes go a day or two,
having either forgotten,
or semi-consciously
rebelling agains't taking
them. But I always go back
on them. With the three
fold pressure and
monitoring from my wife,
community psychiatric
nurse, and dad. And whilst
I may be able to fool one
of them, for some of the

time. The pressure from
all three, has so far, as
yet, always got me back on
them in one piece.

Maybe the closest I came
to a hospital section, was
about a couple of months
ago, where I started
having whole body
fits/spasms, when I took
my tablets, that time. I
don't know why this was,
whether it was a reaction
to the tablets, or perhaps
an interaction with the
scorching sun we had had
over a few days, prior.
But I can assure you, that
it wasn't because of my
imagination, (psuedo-
fits), as I later read on
my notes, that the medics
had put it down to. As if
they weren't real.

The truth be told, I was
considering taking an
over-dose in front of H my
nurse, in order to bloody-
well prove to her that I
wasn't faking it.

But you know who persuaded
me not to ? The Happy
Princess (my own daughter
M). God bless her. She may
well have saved my life
that day.

They did put me on
emergency monitoring from
the actute crisis team for
maybe a week or two, after
this. Which I don't know
if this was just to
monitor me, or if it was
to cover their own backs,
but I got better from this
episode, whatever caused
it.

Thank God. And thankyou
princess.

## Next Chapter :
## Orders

Little Pipa approached her
brother...

« Pipa... »
« Yes sir ? »
« Write a new book, and
that's an order ! »
« Yes Sir ! »
She answered.
« And take good care of
yourself ! »
« Yes sir, yes sir »
She finished.

Life isn't always easy. We
take what we can, when we
can. Some of us break the

law. Some of us get locked
out.

Some of us get a job. Some
of us have families. Make
friends. Some of us do
well, others of us, less
so.

There are some sayings,
which become common
parlance :
Such as : *History repeats
itself.*

*Or learn from your
mistakes, so you don't
repeat them*

*They say we've all got a
book inside us...*

But there is definitely
something to be said, that
'*practice makes perfect*',

So literally the more you
do something, the better
it gets.

And this goes for pretty
much anything. From
playing Xbox/Playstation
games, such as Cod Blops
(Call of duty Black ops),
or GTA V (grand theft auto
five).

The older we get, the
closer we get to death. So
we fight on, to live
another day. But one day
we will all die. One day
all that I will have left,
is this written word.
People will look back at
my life, and wonder.

What was it like for this
man, who had the whole of
his life ahead of him, and

then like that had it all
taken away.

Do we really understand
what goes through the mind
of an individual who is
lost, and stuck in a
vicious circle. In and out
of hospital. Of trouble
with the Feds.

Yesterday I wrote an email
to the Government Select
committee with regards to
a mental health bill
update, they are working
on.

The main focus of this
email was two fold.
Firstly to draw attention
to the fact that the fact
the little people at the
bottom, the families, the
hospital patients, and

dare i say even people who
fall on the wrong side of
the law, need better
juresdiction. I understand
that there are already
safe-guards in place. But
as far as I'm concerned,
these don't go far enough.
And this is from some-one
who spent two year's
straight in hospital, at
the last count. This
simply isn't acceptable,
to my mind. Not for a dad.
Not for a husband.

So guess what, yes i am
still a dad, and i am
still a husband. I didn't
give her a divorce when
she asked for it. I mean
if she really wants one,
there is a way she can get
it, without my knowledge,
or permission. But I'm

hoping it *won't* come to
that.

And the second reason for
writing my books ? Let's
just say there was
something I needed to get
off my chest.

Basically I have heard too
many people in the
streets, calling me nasty
names. And i don't like
this. So i proactively had
to take steps, to deny
this. So that is what I
did.

So what else ? Oh yes, it
looks like i have got a
new job today. Working in
an office, or at least i
have been in to talk to a
manager, about the
possibility of me working
for them. And she seemed

very positive about it.
That was yesterday. This
really boosted my
confidence, and does a lot
to promote my ego, and
happiness. If i'm not
happy, or big-headed
enough, as it is ?

Yesterday was actually
quite a tough day for me.
I wrote that
'confession'/lifestory
document, and printed it
ten times, then dropping
it off around town, to the
police, and other various
points, in the Derby city
centre.

So why did I do this ?
Because I wanted to get it
clear with people, that I
am guilty of some stuff,
but then not others. And

also I wanted to stop the
voices. As i already said.

When I got back in the
evening, I hadn't been
arrested, which was a
start. And i actually felt
exhausted. Today my nurse
came to see me. And she
told me that every-thing
is fine. Well at least she
said something like that.
Or words to that affect.
And she also said that she
is prepared to support me,
in my attempt to ask the
doctor for another
reduction, in my meds,
when i next see her in six
months. I think.

Oh yes, and she also got
married, since i last saw
her. God bless her.

So yes it's like i said,
we make friends, lose
them. Take our time. Some
of us have our time taken
away from us.

Smile when we are happy,
cry when we are sad. Have
babies when we are
fertile, and sit by
ourselves watching
movies/TV/or listen to
music/play games, when we
are not.

Some-body once told me,
that there is some-body
watching over us.

Good-night guys/and
girls/ladies.

# The Internet

Okay let me talk about the
internet for a minute or
two here ;
 Plus let me say, I know
my writing seems to be
taking some natural shape
of its own, by working to
this format, so for
example I start with a
chapter heading, and then
use that to kick off my
thought process ; but
that's okay right ?

We all have our own
prefered formats to write
to. And should you one day
get to write your own
book, I hope that you will
get yours ?

Yes Okay, so the thing
about the internet, is I
have literally been using
it since it was pretty
much first invented. I
mean I remember using it
in 1997 and earlier, to
check my Compuserve
emails, and play Excite
and later Pogo chess.

(None of which now exist
any-more).

These early days of
online-chess were way
before the modern chess
engine, gave every tom
drake and sally, the
powers of a super-computer
at a touch.

And this is to say nothing
of the modern 'cheating'
chess controversies
currently blowing up

between Hans Niemann and
Magnus Carlson the current
world champion. So whilst
it is possible that Hans
cheated, allegedly, I
personally think he has
just adapted a playing
style which beats
computers, and so well he
didn't.

In fact there has not been
an over-whelming consensus
against him, so whilst the
general public opinion,
has tended to side with
the world-champion, and i
do think Niemann is
pushing his luck in trying
to sue Carlson and others
for millions, the jury is
still out on that one.

Any-way, so twenty years
ago, when the modern

generation of chess
masters were just still
wriggler's in their mum
and dad's knickers, we
were playing some of the
greatest games of chess,
man has ever known.

This was before I adopted
the Dutch opening (Queen's
Gambit as White, or K4, Q5
as Black ?!)

Although I probably did
play it a bit, I also
experimented with other
ideas. So for example I
mad the transition from
the King's Gambit, to try
out different ideas.

Chess is still very much
in it's infancy, as far as
I can see. And whilst
computer's are still
developing fast, imagine

how much more the game
will have come on, in the
next twenty years ? If we
are still alive then ? Or
the next hundred, which we
most likely won't be ? Or
thousand, at which point I
can seriously imagine that
the current fad for chess,
and indeed
computer/console games
could well have died out ?
Or then ten thoussnd
years ? At which point
Mankind, if we are still
alive, and haven't wiped
each other out with
atomic/nuclear war-fare,
and most likely fossil
fuels, will be a thing of
the past.

Will clectric hover-cars
be the thing ? Or will we
all be living in super-
citys ? Perhaps ever

beyond the orbit of our
home Earth ?

From all these things,
looking forwards, and
looking back ? How does it
feel ?

Do you still look after
your family ?
Do you still value the
compassion and humanity of
good-ness and charity.

Is love still the pillar
of things.

Or have things descended.
Have things broken up,
broken down. Do you look
back at me writing as some
sad lonely creep. Who
tries to justify his
actions with the power of
the pen, and the judgement
of a prisoner.

Or do you accept that
despite my mistakes, I did
have some credit.

Some validation. Some
jurisdiction. As small as
it may have been.

Thanks for reading.

PS OKAy one more thing.
Back to this whole issue
of the internet. It is
actually a good way to get
our news, and stay in
touch with our loved ones,
be it through Facebook,
Twitter, Whassap, or any
other app.

I don't know if you have
read my ealier books, but
my constant arguments,
online validation and
desecration of the

internet, has been a
pressing issue, across my
other books. And be this
right, or not, I have
greatly advanced by
literary skills, by this
ways.

I would say, that whatever
your generation, or point
in this journey, whether
you are a youth just
beginning to make friends
on here, an old time pro,
such as myself, an ancient
grand-parent, who still
hasn't quite figured out
how to turn your smart-
phone on (such as my mum),
or some-where inbetween,
keep on learning,
experimenting, and moving
forwards. Drive the
narrative. And don't be
stuck in the past.

Sure grieve for what
you've lost. Just try to
find strength where you
can. Love where you can.

God in His almighty glory
has a place on his right
hand side, for you.

And if you don't believe
in Jehovah, mother
nature ? A place by her
side ? Sure down in the
soil, where one day your
body will rot away to. All
of our bodies meet that
same fate, one day.

But your eternal soul,
your heavenly spirit ?
Where does that end up ?

No-one knows for sure.
They say Faith isn't a
science, more an art. But

sciences, and the arts,
are complementary, right ?

Forget about SchrÖedinger
and his cats for a minute,
I want to take you back
further, back to the
Greeks. Nimzovich with his
epic 'The Birth of
Tragedy' which challenged
all prior wisdom of the
Greek pantheon's hierachy,
and asked us to look once
again to the divine, of a
thousand year prior.

How we can look for a
definition, when all we
have is theory and the
fragments of evidence.
Specifically the arguments
of the diety's Appollo
(The God of War), and
Dionysus (The God of
Wine). The idea that this
two immortals, could wrest

their eternal battle, in
the face of humanity, and
that there could only be
one winner.

War is not fought over
deserts. But whether a
winner will be
established, or whether a
truce, is the better out-
come. Should for example,
one side refuse to back
down, until he loses all
public respect, and the
decency of the Gods, as
indeed happened in
Vietnam. Which the West
didn't lose a single
battle, but by their sheer
tenacity and disgraceful
annihilation of the
civilian population on the
ground, lost the war. As
indeed we lost the war in
Iraq, in much the same
war.

Because I don't care what
side you are on, the idea
that you can 'attack'
another sovereign country,
kill a million plus of
their civilians (Google it
if you don't believe me),
and still walk away with
your head held high, is
just a lie you tell
yourself.

We've all got blemishes on
our records. Thankfully,
that one isn't on mine.

Good-night, God-bless !


## A bit wet


Do you know what, that's a
bit wet. I mean people do
like to read inbetwixt the

lines, and I'll be damned
if i don't know how to
prempt guys and girls, cos
I have been writing from
under the radar for so
long now.

But I also think, If i can
just summon up a dash of
that madness, that is now
something of my
trade+mark, a madness
which carried me over and
through my books,
previously, and on to a
new chapter of my life.

You know only a few months
ago, and I fired some
opening warning shots at
my dad, over coffee, in
some local coffee shops,
in town i mean. I mean I
really lost it with him, I
snapped, and shouted the
house down. Like LEAVE

IT ! On y va. Merde. Yes,
etc. (If you know how to
speak french, then good
for you. I on y va, means,
« Go on » and merde means
« Shoot » Anyway I
digress.

Yes so i shouted at him.
Looking back I actually
think they put something
in the coffee, which drugs
me out of reality. And
means that I am less well
hinged to stay grounded.
This is a possibility,

Look I'm sorry if you
think what i'm saying is
b.s. or just lies, but I'm
speaking the Truth. My
Truth. And i want you to
repect that. Anyway.

Yes so i think they put
drugs in my coffee.
Shouted at my dad.

Damn it, I've hugged
people who i shouldn't
have. Had god knows how
many families. And
struggle to hold on to
this one.


People who condemn me for
this ? Well maybe you have
never been married. Maybe
you never took that risk.
Settling down is a big
step. And not all of us
can stay married, when we
do it. What was it Donald
Trump that got married,
three times ?

And Even Bill Gates, one
of the richest men in the
world, well he had to give

his wife a divorce when
she asked for it.

Anyway.

Yes so thanks for bearing
with me. I know I may not
always meet up to your
expectations. Your
understanding of what it
is to be a carried,
presentablem fufilled, and
strong man. Not
androdynous.

Okay I may not be very
good at that. Like when I
blow my top, i just shout
really loud.

Or when I ejaculate, I go
soft and shrink, real
quick after.

True. Sure, I know it
sucks, You wanted to be

ridden like a horse for
longer, to be carried
through the twelve gates
of female orgasmic heaven,
and i took you to the
first one, then boggered
off.

Haha.

Never-mind,

Look darling, I did my job
okay.

Whether you choose to
carry him, or her inside
you to term, the full nine
months,

kill him or her (abort)

,

and when born, have him
taken from you, or raise
him successfully,

I suppose that depends on
your own family network,
extended family, or maybe
I shouldn't be saying
this.

I know some men can have
and pay for multiple
children. Good for them.

But as I said already, I
struggle to upkeep my just
one/


Actually no, that is a lie
as well.

She has been a blessing
ever since the day she was
born.

Ever since she read her
first book to me.

So that is something as
least.
Good-night.

Grandpa Major Cliff
Simmons

# Dedicated to the
dead: Rest in
Peace

Captain Clifford A.
Simmons General Surgeon,
Obstetrician and
Gynaecologist, Notes and
Records
Chapter One: Medical
Notebook (1940?)

Dear Messieur
    I have moved into
Worcester hall. I shall
need some sheets & pillow
slips & towels. Say 3
sheets, 2 pillow cases + a
couple of towels. If you
have room also my electric
bellts (if you don't need
it is *in* the cellar, but
don't worry if you do, I
can use the coal fire)

Parsue tue
I was going to call at
keeble at 7:30 to see if

either Joan (as she at)
were coming out for a
drink or flick (*movie*) (if
were not going out with
Cliforde).
What are you doing after
supper you might call for
them (or her) & meet me in
a pub after the wather has
produced.

(a) Ok
(b) What time do you think she will
produce
(c) What pub
(d) I don't know what Chips is
doing.


I'll phone chiscatly after
this lecture – for it
then.

6 Baby takes breast
greedily, swallows milk in
great gulps. After 1 or 2
minutes it becomes
restless and cries for ai
(*love*) and food
Slow down feeding Boiled
water before disgrace 1
offord if bad.
Interrupt feed allow baby
to lay off wind.

Breast ditiery – sudden
and fast conflase
Teat
Tears
False

//insert diagram here,
scan//


Gland diet Inflammatory
Baby cold not breathing

The baby is born with the
heart beating well and
will never breathe et
large clot is formed from
blood from sinus & lat
sinus by flasis & late if
use tears

Alternative = Risking 1
baby sinus = wefaire
The R.P.S. nuffille
Laeniorolger
Some babies lots of sick
if with feed
Lateslief also babies with
long tracts may be
breechs.

Sunday 17<sup>th</sup> Sept. '44
It really is on this time,
or it's the biggest
exercise yet.
No.2. Light Section
emplane with jeep and
handcart. Weather good –
broken cumulus. Air
warming up ….. it'll be
bumpy.
Three lines of Horses each
a mile long swing in turn
behind their
tugs and away into a West
wind takeoff. Arnhem..
Rhine town of
Holland. Remember the
landing zone.
Wood..stubble land, bombed
barracks and a farm , just
where the electric railway
running from

the West divides outside
the town itself. Should be
easy to spot.

Time….? Flying West over
Canterbury, a turn
Northward 180°
and then due East back
over Manston, Margate,
turning slightly , a
few degrees Northward and
then out over the North
sea with it's bottom
plainly visible from this
height.

Dropping below the
tugplane for height. The
formation has grown
magically..didn't notice
the link up.

One glider in the sea with
A.S.Rescue
alongside...reassuring
sight.

Dutch coast low on the
horizon. A few scattered
islands on the Hook.
Over the mainland which is
very badly flooded. This
is new we had
Not heard of this. (
Should have been obvious
really)

The lashings on the jeep
settle down with a loud
crack. Obvious
Consternation covered by
even more obvious sang
froid.

Somebody must be shooting
from this peaceful, scene
below ..a glider
has just gone straight in.
Funny but this doesn't
seem like war to
me. I had pictured it
before but this is more
like travelling to an

important football
fixture...with the same
fellows too. Crazy...too
peaceful.   6,000 feet
I'd guess, still flying
through light
wisps of cloud.

Must be getting well
inside Holland now. Two
sunken barges in a
Canal. Tow 'Spits' and a
'Tiffy' are hammering away
at a third
Diving straight in and
swinging away from the
bottom of their dives
up and over. Didn't see
what happened we're past
now. Terrific.

That's a warning from the
pilot, must be near the
L.Z. A few minutes

Yet.    Peculiar whistling
"zagging" noise. That's a
hole somewhere
Probably the wing fabric.
Puffs of fleck. Look
harmless.    The Rhine
Lower branch,     No the
Maas.    Some more flack
but still very light.
Can't see the front of the
formation now, probably
breaking up to
land.    Another river..the
Waal I think.    Packing
this up must be
near…. A tug has just gone
back past us with loose
tow rope  we're
there O.K.   A river passed
beneath, a large sized
town..tilting down
Farm buildings. House
burnin g.. also barracks
further over,   Horses

Running across the ground
seemingly in every
direction.

( I got this far with a
fairly accurate 'Running
commentary' but events
from now on were written
at odd moments in the most
unlikely places,
and I definitely do not
vouch for xxxxxxxxxxxxxxx
the accuracy of
time or place from here
on)

(Written Sunday evening in
a barn on L.Z/)
Made good landing after
usual approach. Surface
loose loam, ploughed.
Mac's (Pte.McGowan's) seat
collapsed with shock of
landing. Left

hanging in straps cussing
horribly.  Just what was
needed to break
the tension. I felt better
at once.  Tail had to be
chopped away
and finally fell on G.P's
back. Our first casualty.
Jeep out in
good order but "Safety"
split pins in "quick"
release mechanism seemed
to have got opened and
folded down flat onto the
release. After
reporting
at'concentration'point
and getting a stand down
order we do
a quick sweep of wrecked
Gliders.  Occupants had
either walked away
or bought it *(died)*.
Mortar bursts 30 feet
overhead, fairly
concentrated

but appear futile.  Our
lift is all down….we were
pretty well the last.

   Clean up glider that
had the misfortune to land
in front of
M.G. site. Two dead, six
wounded, Capt ? fractured
xxxx humerous,
right, clothing badly
burned.  Jeeped over the
M.D. at Wolfheze in
good time.  Wireless
notification of further
casualties in D.Z.
South of the Railway.  Did
not contact ofter wide
sweep.

Large rubber tyred farm
cart attached to rear of
Jeep as extra rolling
stock, definitely not
successful. We needed a
rigid all-purpose tow-bar.
                      Mor
tar bomb lands on
"trailer" and settles all
further argument.    We
leave at double.

Back to Farm and hang on
with No.2 Light section
and assortment of R.E.'s
and Sigs and a few Staffs.

(Written in emergency
"staging" Aid post between
ARNHEM and the M.D.S.
Night,Monday)

Stayed at farm all that
night (Sunday) and moved
off at about midday.

Little doing.  Civilians
brought in for
questioning, a few dead to
be attended too with the
aid of the Padre.   He
asked for help just
as if he wanted some hymn
books given out at a
Service. Still seems
unreal.   We discuss the
tanks we heard moving in
the night,  sounded
quite near but probably a
long way off.
Hand cart loaded together
with Jeep, and at about
noon we moved off across
country to the main road,
taking tree cover.

First news that resistance
in the town is greater
than anticipated.
Pass M.D.S. at Wolfheze ,
the village and station
wrecked. Bombimg.

Had our first taste of
attention from above on
this road to Oosterbeek.
We were rather
"concentrated" but there
is plenty of foliage
overhead.
I have always liked
trees...I loved them then.
There were about ten
Bandits, an assortment of
190's , 109's and a
captured Spit, also I
think a 'jet'. These
staged an effective shoot-
up with a hell of a
lot of noises off, but
none of the lads gave
experience of finding any
casualties from this
attack.

S/Sgt. Cpl. and the two
Ptes detached from section
to set up receiving

station for casualties in
a cottage just off this
road just before it
contacted the main road
into Costerbeek and
Arnhem. At this junction
we found a Jerry staff car
shot to pieces, to say
nothing of the occupants.
All four were high ranking
officers and we passed
their papers over to
the Padre.    Several of
our chaps had caught it
here.    One apparently
carrying a mine which was
detonated by a hit.

By 20.00hrs. our station
is full and the two Jerry
prisonners we collected
(about 20 yrs and 40yrs
old) gave willing help.
They appear rather

dazed, which does seem
understandable. Evacuation
going smoothly but
shortage of jeeps felt
occasionally.

The time of writing now is
24.00 (sorry..23.49)  We
are full up with
unevacuated casualties.
The M.D.S. went past us
towards Oostrtbeek,
late evening, and we have
heard nothing from then
since.   This place
is getting knocked to
pieces by M.G. fire from
all sides.   Our chaps
are dug in outside.
Hell, what a row!

The second lift came in
today (Monday) don't know
time..about midxxx-

afternoon.    Much heavier
flack. Found our way back
to L.Z. and saw
several Amilcar gliders
fail in the loose loam.
Dug their noses in
and went right over.   L.Z.
under M.G. fire. Did all
possible in circs.
but everybody seemed to be
fighting everybody else.
Xxxxx I am sure
some Poles were shooting
xx at us.   One outstanding
casualty. Para-
trooper landed in gorse
and was taken cross
country by his chute
because
the release box was
tangled in gorse vine.
Skin dragged off hand to
finger tips.     Seemed to
go back O,K, after a clean
op.

We are using A.G.G. serum
on all casualties
'regardless'. I am sick
of the sight of rumps.
The famous tyreless
ambulance has paid us
another visit *(death?)*,
and eased
the overcrowding, it is
now merely three times
normal.
The owner of this coattage
has just returned xxxx and
us living in the
one back room. Quite co-
operative.----------------
-----------------------

(Following written in
Appeldoorn)

Tuesday (19th.)
Shipped all patients on to
M.D.S. by commandeered
transport.
Visit by plain clothed
Dutchman (just after

finishing entry Monday
night)
who claimed to have jumped
with the 2$^{nd}$. Lift, asking
shelter. We passed
him on to owner of cottage
who knew him personally as
a "local" who had
escaped to England.
No contact with M.D.S.
We seemed to have come
adrift from our mob. But
there
was bags of equipment and
plenty to do.
By 10.00hrs infiltrating
patrols had been pushed
back and we were able
to pack up and clear out
as our line started to
bend backwards onto the
town.
It was about 5 or 6 miles
to Costerbeek and the road
was still under

mortar fire. A/T was set
up facing West along the
road.
Made Costerbeek in record
time and reported to
M.D.S.
Were informed here that it
would not be possible to
contact rest of our
light Section and
instructed to report at
Overflow "meeting" in
hotel
across the street.
Here we met one other
member of our Section
organising enthusiastic
but
Amateurish civilian
stretcher bearers, to
carry cases from main
M.D.S.
to the hotel.
By mid-night we have the
place as normal as it
could be. Three fully

equipped wards working
quietly and efficiently.
Patients comfortable.

Wednesday (20th)
Wards operating well with
aid of Dutch nurse "Janie"
(Sorry to say I never
had time to get her
address)    One patient
died 08.00hrs. (This was
the
first of a total of three)
for the whole time the
M.D.S. held this building

Thursday (21st)
Cross roads outside under
heavy mortar fire.  Our
glass covered corridor
outside the front wall of
the building was wrecked
within twenty minutes
of being cleared of
patients.

Patients surrender what
mattresses they possess to
fix in front of windows.
Casualty sweep produced
large airborne rubber
dingy which we inflated
and filled with drinking
water while the supply
still held.
Another important
collection during the same
sweep was a German officer
with splintered "fib and
tib" because he stood us
in good stead when later
in the day an isolated
German patrol moved in.
We were joined at lunch
time (the word lunch is
obviously a misnomer) by
the remains of a
17th.th.Para F.A. section
who had been occupying a
nearby

school which had been
demolished by a heavy
shell, killing all their
patients and most of their
parsonnel.   One of their
men a Cpl.Cooley
took over as senior
N.C.O.,most efficiently.
We used A.G.G. serum in
each case.(It is worth
mentioning that not a
single
case of Gangrene developed
as a result of this serum)
We now had the misfortune
to get tangled up in a A/T
V Tiger affray
during a casualty sweep
and lost trace  of three
of our precious staff
who were not able to get
back with us.  As a
compensation we were able
to

collect from a house, 24
packets of 24hr. Rations,
a sack of tea, and a
sack of sugar.
German patrol moved in
during the late afternoon
and were later pushed out
again. During the
occupation one of the
invaders punctured our
make-shift
reservoir but on
complaining to their
N.C.O. they patched and
re-inflated
it.    Lights shortly
afterwards gave up the
unequal struggle, but
there
was a plentiful supply of
torches.
Bomb landed just outside
French doors. Patients
were laying below blast

line and were O.K.  We
patched up the holes and
re swung the door, and
spent rest of night
exhuming pieces from the
orderly in the Ward at the
time.  He was not at all
appreciative.
Had our first visit by a
Medical Officer who set a
dislocated shoulder
and moved on.  Everything
else quite O.K.
Late that afternoon we
found a G.P. with what
appeared at the time to be
severe G.S.W. of the
abdomen.  He refused to
allow us to treat him and
walked
back with us. Later
investigation showed that
a heavy bullet had torn
the flesh away in a 6″
long furrow, uncovering

the intestine which did
not
come out of position so
that we were able to clean
and dress the wound
which I now know to have
healed well. During the
whole time with us as a
patient he refused to let
go of his empty Sten gun
which we were forced

THE PETERBOUG CONFERENCE
after the 8 days
conference has haled by
1777 drations Churchill
and Roosevelt at Jacia
(Crimea) the following
communications have
been issued mischeviously
at London, Herciou and
Warhinghan
if Point : Germany's
Defeat . all strategic
details have been
fixed , The operation
directed against Germany's
Centere will be stacked
from East, West, South and
North. It is the evilerest
of the
German Nation to avemge
the War . The evilerallied
of Q. melting
every day.

2/ <u>beaufafies and administrations</u> . Germany will be obliged to surrender without cavelltion. The justification will be published only after the defeat. Each of the 3 Parcuers will occupy depuite Jenir administration will 'be conschinivated by central amikee established at Jenkin. France will participate in the occupation under the same conditions . The Gainfiset commission ,
The Reich will have to repair the damages, a commitee for this question is established at Marcois.

3/ <u>Destruction of Nazi
System</u> . We are decidesnt
to destroy gaims of
Milihaiiesm and Nazism .
Never again Germany must
be a
danger for Peace. The
german great general staff
will have to
disappear. all military
activity will be
voileidalei : War
industries and factories
hansformiable who was
industries
will be destroyed. Nazi
organisations, party, laws
will
be riffierryed. That way
we will give the german
people a
fair chance of reasonable
chance paciful life .
4/ <u>Problems of Liberated
Eurp[e .</u> We are decided to
aid

the liberated Nations and
Germany's former allies to
entadlisk Democracy. We
will help civil
populations be able
go to/the vote soon.
5/ <u>Polish problem</u> We will
contribute to form a fine.
strong
and independent Poland
under a national union
cabinet
as soon as possible free
elections will be held
where
all autinage factories
heass present covids
'deihes' The
Eastern frontier will be
constitutede by the ciuzan
line
with the exeption of some
spots where the line will
best
in favour of Poland by to
5 miles. Poland will

reuse an counter fact in
North and West ,
6/ YOUGOSLAVIA . The
government is invited to
exeruk a
seen as terrible the
substitute in the
agreement. It is dismissal
that members of the old
cabinet who did not
collaborate with
Germany may enter the new
government.
7/ Further meeting every 3
for 4 months. the 3chiefs
will meet in the different
capitals. The next
confidence
will be held at London .
8/ Peace organisation The
principals established at
Dumbaiber Oath will be
eliminated at an
enterabled

conference to be held at
San Francisco the 15<sup>th</sup> of
april
France and China will be
invited immediatly and
will be
asked to give their advice
on invilelious to the
adressed
to offer goverments
9/ <u>Collaboration</u> which has
lead to victory will be
strengthened
in the future to reolise
excluding peace and to
protect
humanity from war, misery
and fear _
    <u>Complimentary</u> details

_
The foreign minister , the
chiefs of the general
staff, and
difleimalie experts were
present, _

M. Churchill has arrived
at false summertime before
the
opening of the conference
–
The French government, and
the Polish government at
London
have been informed of all
questions concerning their
interests
all military, political
and economical questions
have been
examinable detailed.
an agreement has been
signed concerning
arisbause to, an
repadiation of, allied
P.O.W. liberated during
the campaign.

ARMED FORCES
AIR MAIL
TORONTO
MAR 30

4.30 PM
1944
ONTARIO
If anything is enclosed in
this letter it will be
sent by ordinary mail.

TO: CAPTAIN C. A. SIMMONS,
R.A.M.C.,
181 A/C.Landing, Field
Ambulance,
HOME FORCES, ENGLAND

FROM:
Miss EVELYN SIMMONS,
32 Dewhurst Boulevard,
TORONTO, Ontario,
CANADA.

32 Dewhurst Boulevard,
Toronto 1, Ontario.
March 29th, 1944.

Captain C. A.Simmons:

Dear Captain Simmons:-

We were so very
surprised to receive your
letter
saying you had received
two parcels of cigarettes
intended for
our brother.  When we saw
your name on the back of
the letter.
Captain, we thought he had
been demoted.  His name is
Major
Cyril A. Simmons,
D.A.D.M.,
R.C.A.S.C.
Canadian Section, G.H.Q.,
1 Ech., Adv. A.F.H.Q.,
C.M.F.
He is now stationed in
Italy.
I think it was
very nice of you to have
tried to
get the parcels to reach
him and being unsuccessful
to have

let us know.  We
appreciate it very much
and would like you to
keep one parcel for
yourself and send the
other on.
Are you English
or Canadian, by any
chance.
Clifford sounds English.
How are you liking the
war?  It is
lasting much too long.
Cy. has been over since
May, 1940.
He is now the Deputy
Assistant Director of
Movement.  He spent
nine months in Alexandria,
Cairo, Tunis, Palestine,
Persia, etc.,
then went back to C.M.H.Q.
in London and left for
Italy last July.

Thanks once
again-Captain-and please
keep one
parcel of cigarettes for
yourself, if they are not
too stale,
and you could, if it is
not too much trouble, sent
the other
on to Cy. at the above
address.

Yours very truly,
Evelyn Simmons Signed

Subject:- Volunteer
R.A.M.C. for Airbourne
Units.
A,D.M.S.,
Algiers Area.
     Ref: M.146/S
dated 11th June, 1943.
     Sir,
     I have the
Honour to volunteer for
Service as Medical
Officer in an Airbourne
Unit.
     Lieut. C.A.
Simonds,R.A.M.C., No.
250323. Medical Officer
in No. 7 Docks Group,
R.M., Algiers. Age 25.
Military Service 6 months.
EDUCATION.
     St. Paul's
School, Kensington.
Wadham College, Oxford.

Qualified B.A.,
B.M., B.Ch. from Redcliffe
Infirmary, Oxford
March, 1942.
HOSPITAL EXPERIENCE.
Six months House
Surgeon to the Senior
Surgeon of the
Royal Sussex
County Hospital, Brighton.
Surgical reference
enclosed.
EXPERIENCE IN R.A.M.C.
Commission
October 31st. 1942
Months cource at
No. 1 Depot R.A.M.C.,
Crookham.
1 weeks course
Hygene at School of
Hygene, Mytchett.
Posted to
Edinburgh, and spent
several weeks working

for Military
Hospital, Edinburgh
Castle, on one occassion
        running a C.R.S.
(20 beds).
        Posted to No. 7
Docks Group, R,M., after a
2 weeks course
        at the School of
Tropical Medicine,
Liverpool.


RPOPRS & HOSPIRS
        Member of Oxford
University & City Gliding
Club, holding
        Glider Pilots
Licence A & B.
        College Rowding
Colours (1$^{st}$ rowding
colours).
        School 1$^{st}$
Fencing Colours.
        Ski_ing Fair
ability.

I tried for
Service in the Airbourne
Division within a month
of joining the R,A.M.C.
My application was
formerly refused a few
days before
doing my Tropical Medicine
Course.
I was then
examined and found fit for
service in an Airbourne
Division but had lost some
weight owding to an attack
of Infective Hepatitis
one week after being
Commiissioned.    I am now
quite fit.
I have the
Honour to be, Sir,
Your
obedient servant,


Lieut, R.A.M.C.

Field.
/June/43

16<sup>th</sup> FEB 43

R. A. MESS,
REDFORD BARRACKS,
          EDINBURGH, 13.
TEL. COLINTON 872101.

February 16<sup>th</sup> 1943

Dear Mamma + Dad
          Many thanks for
the key – I
hope that it will not be
too long before
I use it again.
I've settled down (almost)
once more, to
the dreary routine of Army
life + have my
own medical room to attend
to in the
mornings + go to the
castle + do nothing
in the afternoons.
Actually the high slot

of this afternoon was
going to a Maternity
Hospital + interviewing a
pregnant A.T,S!
        I saw an old
friend of mine from
Oxford in the streets this
morning but as I was
on top of the trass I was
unable toattend his
address – I'll try + find
him later in
the week.


              2.
I believe the weather is
considered mild
here – It was rather
chilling to look out
of the train window, on
the journey up + finf
it all frosted up.
        Captain
Gibson, the old M.O, at
Redford

has been promoted + moved
into town + the
M.O who has taken his
place is a good lad, a
bit with an 'Oxford
accent' (he comes from
near Oxford). We get on
quite well.
All the
other lads have left
(Brugand
+ Borris who were with me
at first). They
are both acting as M.O's
to AcAc.
Has Ted
arrivid home yet? Thank
him for his letters when
he does_ I'll
write to him later in the
week.
Of course I
had nothing; to do thus
Sunday I arrived back _
andall sit in

a room for 3 hours _ which
I do
every afternoon,
            My application
for Airborne has
been rejected_ I am
furious but I am
afraid that there is
nothing that I
can do about it.

3.
Did Jenning turn up on
the Wednesday?
Or did the chiastiabian
Flight Sergt. cHam
cHoley, That I met last
Sunday; those ?
He was a very nice lad + I
am reviewing
my opinions of the
Australians.
          I'm afraid that I
have no more news
at the moment so till
later,
          love Cliff.

          Love to all the
family.

1. <u>Object.</u> To practise i. Digging and Marching.

2. <u>Troops taking part.</u> As detailed in Part 1 Orders Serial 17 A dated 12 Jul 44.

3. <u>Duration.</u> 24 – 28 July 44. inclusive.

4. <u>Programme.</u>
24 July   Road move to MOSSY LEE 525151
   Start    1400 hrs
   Route.

STE NIGOF _ MARKET RASEN A GAINSBOROUGH _ RAUTRY _ TICKHILL _ SHEFFIELD _ GLOSSOP.

Vehicles.            4 x
3 tonners (RASC)
2 x 15 owt.
1 Ambulance equipped.

25 July
Reveille        0600
hrs,

Breakfast 0700 hrs.
March      0800 hrs.
Route      Track running
B. S. B. to road at 563133,  road
to area
            E of 608100,
bivouac night 25/26.
26 July  Reveille    0700 hrs.
        Breakfast  0800 hrs.
        March      0900 hrs.
        Route      Left fork
618096, turn EAST at
LOCKERBROOK FARM road

junction
638098 – Rd junction 641099 –
and E cross-

country to
track 653115 – cross-roads
70322 _ rd

junction
730121 – cross-roads 705127 –
track 750125.

Bivouac
night 16/27 N of convent.

27 July    Reveille    0530 hrs

Breakfast  0630 hrs

March      0730 hrs

Move by M. T.  0530
hrs.

Transport to 581203 –
cross-country – pt 2061 (Div
5516. –

MOSSY LEE.

Return to STENGOT by
M. T.    Route as out-going.

5.      Dress.
Exercise Order;  denims and berets.   Bed Rolls will include spare
boots and steel helmets.

6.      Equipment. All available picks and shovals, section compasses and watches and
binoculars, 2 No. 1 Cookers, 4 x 6 gall. containers, 6 kettles camp and cooks
implements.   No medical equipment.

7.      Ratiens.   Unexpired portions of 23 July rations for 24 July will be taken.

8.      Discipline.  Airbourne discipline has not been good in this area; the

discipline of this unit will be its usual standard.  Sanitary discipline is of
highest importance as this is a catchment area.

23 July 44.
          Lieut.Col.,
R.A.M.C.,
RCT.       Commanding 161
dir Landing Field
Ambulance.

R. A. MESS,
REDFORD BARRACKS,
EDINBURGH, 13.
TEL. COLINTON 872101.

March 21st 1943

Dear Mamma & Dad,
    Just a line to say
that I
have been having a week-
end holiday and
am still on Inchcolon : at
small island
near the Forth Bridge. I
arrived here
yesterday morning at some
unhealthy
hour to relieve the M/O &
I return
tomorrow, back once more
to the castle (I
am afraid.)
    There is a very early
old abby

here which is very
interesting & I am
going to loke arround it
this afternoon.
    I have collected most
of my

2.

camp kit – chair, bath,
bed, aso-called
valise, which is just a
sleeping bag, very
utility and odds & ends.
God knows how
I am going to travel.
      I am getting resigned
to my fate
here, once more & find it
impossible to
read vary much.
      One very bright shot
on returning
has been setting in (and)
my room
at Radford & contemplating
the again that
you gave me. Dad. I have
already
smoked half) then – very
good too

A bit late
but I have been very busy.
3/5/43
Love Cliff
Regards to George
& Geof.

Simmons          RIO: 2331.
          30. 7. 43

Dear Mamma and Dad.
          I received a
letter from Jean yesterday
which broke the news. Your
letter arrived today, and
has taken
a long time over the
journey.  It has made me
very sad. I'm afraid,
although I guessed Vera
was failing, when I said
"good-bye" to her.
          We shall all miss her
very much, and if you have
a
"sen of" of Vera & Aown, I
should love to have one.
You must not make too
much fuss of little down-
you know Grand Parents
always do.  Thank Goodness

for her! I can imagine her
chubby smiling cheeks now,
and only
wish she could take me out
for a coulk.     You know
that
things are much more
worrying when one is away
from home. I am
sure that you need it.
        I shall be
writing to Ted and the
Rouses in a day
or so. Poor old Ted. I
should like to have taken
him out for a drink.
        I was very relieved
to hear that miss
Rashbrooks brother
was well and alive.
        I am still fairly
busy, but start cashier in
the money now; boys on
sick bay. 8 am sick fasude
8.45  Dad sick fasude.
Letter one requested

_for help by 12 & odd sick
who dad is and out:    Lunch
in the house &
a rest on the bed on again
of "crib" & I return to
the folk at any time
between
2-3. Defending; after
what's on.        We don't
have tea, now I quite

Dislike eating; anything
in the afternoon but I
manage to "sof into"
the meal before & I got a
cup which is very welcome.
    Yesterday I took 4
lads from different
companies outside
the town to see the arte;
mosquitoe looks that was
going on. I felt
rather like Mr Park out
old biology masters at
school_ but I am
afraid that my pupils are
not so keen as we were! We
had a very good trip _
about 30 miles around the
countryside stopping
at 3 different water-beds.
    There is a saint
possibility that I may
return to England for
some training but the odds
are very much against it .

Jean's letter
yesterday gave me all the
news about
Brighton & she seems to
have had a good week-end
at the Royal Sussex County
Hospital .
I've made some very
good friends here and
should bring some
of them home to add to
your troubles after the
war.   They are a
 I'll write some more news
          later on.
   Give my love to all,
          Cliff .
good crowd on the whole. I
shall not like leaving
them if I get
moved.
P.S  I'll send you a small
sketch from my balcony as
soon as
it is finished.
Cliff.

My later, Dad, of getting
that 6<sup>th</sup> of yger dean to
the <u>British Pluon also
freed?</u>

BY AIR MAIL
AIR LETTER
IF ANYTHING IS ENCLOSED
THIS LETTER WILL BE SENT
BY ORDNINARY MAIL.
PASSED BY CENSOR NO. 7601
LONDON W. C. D 11.15 AM 30
AUG
POSTAGE REVENUE 3D

~~M. R. Simmons Esq.~~
~~167 Elect Struct~~
~~London.~~
~~England.~~

10 YEALM HOTEL,
NEWTON FERRERS,
S. DEVON

<u>AUGUST 43</u>
250323, Lt Simmons RAMC
181 Sir London; Field
Ambulance,
B. N. A. F.

Dear Dad,
    Many thanks for your
letter I
16/8/43. It arrived
23/8/43. I have
just had a very tiring
morning – I
met a very sweet young
infirmière
the other day & have had
dinner with
her every night since – I
rose at
05.30 hrs this morning to
see her off
as she is mobilised for
service abroad!
    Since then I have
been chasing

from one office to another
trying
to get on transport (I
have to
go about 600 miles to my
new unit). I am only
priority
iii   so I may have to
queue
at the airodrome for some
while.

Would you please be good
enough to circulate mes
amis
avec mon address novelle_
I
*(my friends' with my new
address)*
shall be a bit nearer to
Don
but not near enough.
Should I
be returning; home for
training; I
will let you know.
       The lads here are
very good
& have been giving me a
good
send off _ I have all
their
addresses & hope to get
some free!
Iliaciauce cruises after
the war
on their boats.

          I have now been
nicknamed
"le serpent" as a month
ago I dinanly
as introdution to the
sister I
our miss secretary's girl
friend _
he wouldn't give it, so at
the last
dance I introduced myself.

        Annie Sheales a
little English but
mostly French.  Her father
is Danish
_ naturalized French,
mother is
French _ altogether "very"
charming _
unfortunately I have only
known her
5 days & if you know the
French
Families at all _ 5 days
is
definitly not long enough.
        I'm swimming with
another
Anne today _ a French Red
Cross
Ambulance driver & here
very
attractive half English
girl friend.
They gave me a lift 20
kilometers

when I had a flatture the
other
day, in their ambulance.
    Love to Mamma - Ted,
chris
Jean_ George & Geibre,
Clarito - love Cliff.

P.S. I treated a Canadian
Csar Gnresfordut, who
knows the Dress Club well.
He is coming to
look you up, when he gets
to town- Cliff. Simmons

ON THIS DAY
April 14, 1945
TYHUS CAUSES A TRUCE
BRITISH TO GUARD
PRISON CAMP
From Our Special
Correspondent
ON THE ALLER, April 13
The full horror of Belsen
was only
realised when British
troops entered the
concentration camp on
April 15, 1945,
one day after this report
was published

By negotiations
between British and Ger-
man officers during a
local truce British troops
will take over from the
S.S. and the
Wehrmacht the guarding the
vast concentra-

tion camp at Belsen, a few
miles north-west of
Celle, which contains
about 60,000 prisoners,
both criminals and anti-
Nazis.

This extraordinary
step has been agreed by
the British because typhus
is rampant in the
camp and it is vitally
necessary that no
prisoners should be
allowed out until the
infection is checked.
Moreover, it will be
necessary for allied
security officers to sort
out
which of the prisoners are
in the camp for
political reasons and
which are serving
sentences for crime.

Under the final
agreement the advancing

British agree to refrain
from bombing and
shelling the area in which
the camp is situated
and the Germans agree to
leave behind an
armed guard for a week
after the British have
arrived. The German
soldiers will afterwards
be allowed to return to
their lines.

The story of the
negotiation is a curious
one.
Yesterday morning two
German officers
presented themselves
before our outposts.
They explained that there
were 9,000 sick in
the camp and that all
sanitisation had failed.
They suggested that the
British should occupy

the camp at once,
declaring that the respon-
sibility was
international, in the
interests of
health. In return for the
delay caused by the
truce, Germans offered to
surrender intact the
bridges at Winsen over the
the River Aller.

  After brief
consideration the British
senior
officer rejected the
German proposals, saying
that the British should
occupy an area of 10
kilometres round the camp
to be sure of

keeping their troops and lines of communication away from the disease. The Germans said they must refer to their senior officer, and a British brigadier and a captain set off to the German HQ. There the German senior officer then rang up Himmler as Reichsführer, whose chief of staff rejected the terms. The new agreement was then concluded. The truce, which had been confined to the area round the Winsen bridge, expired after 12 hours. The Germans blew up the bridge and a very odd interlude in the battle of Germany ended.

RUSSIANS TAKE VIENNA
Marshal Stalin, in an
order of the day
addressed to Marshal
Tolbukhin and Lieuten-
ant-General Ivanov, last
night announced:-
Troops of the 3$^{rd}$
Ukrainian front, in
cooperation with troops of
the 2$^{nd}$ Ukrainian
Front, after stubborn
fighting to-day captured
the city of Vienna, a
strategic strong-point
covering the approaches to
southern
Germany. From March 16 to
April 13 more
than 130,000 prisoner were
taken.
During the battles on
the approaches to
Vienna troops of the 3$^{rd}$
Ukrainian Command

routed 11 tank divisions,
including the 6$^{th}$ S.S.
Tank Army. They also
destroyed or captured
1,345 tanks and self-
propller guns, 2,250 field
pieces, and much other war
equipment.
*A few miles from
Fulindrosted.*

## Guitar

Okay, that comes to the
end of this book. I wish
you guys the best of luck,
in whatever you do, and
wherever you go.

If you choose to do a
degree, great good luck. I
did it. And if I could do
it, any-one could right ?

If you choose to raise a
family. Also great-luck. A
family is the best
challenge and achievement,
in any woman' hell any
man's life. To raise them
from walking, to talking,
to potty trained, to
school, making friends,
and graduation.

We have to raise our next
generations, so they,
those who inherit the
Earth after us, can have
an easier time of it, then
we did.

Play computer games. Hold
down' a job. Learn an
instrument. Learn a
language ? Mon dieu. C'est
trop facile, pour les
escargots, mais pour les
simples gens, comme moi et
toi, comme vous pardons,

c'est assez difficiles,
des temps, mais bof. C'est
ton vie, ton ames. Prix
cette chance avec
doucement, Merci.

Which is to say it is your
life. Take it, as you can.
Step by step. Baby steps
right ?

Our future is in the
stars. Will we ever make
it that far/ Before
death ? Or does our fate
remain locked on this ball
of mud, and fire ?

Even I can't predict that'
i'm afraid.

I've been toying with
ideas for the title of
this book ?
What's in a title, Romeo
cast down to his besotted

Juliet, as she gently
gazed down at him, from
out-side her window
balcony. Curtains gently
blowing in the breeze.
What's in a name. A rose,
by any other name, would
smell as sweet ?

But there's the rub.
Because roses, don't
actually smell of
anything. I think you are
getting them mixed up with
Hyacynths, which do,
truly, smell the world.

Good-night Ladies and
Gentleman. Please forgive
me.

Printed in Poland
by Amazon Fulfillment
Poland Sp. z o.o., Wrocław
22 November 2022

ace2d973-3d5a-4a5d-8f3c-3f98e06bca1eR01